RUGGLES

For Mary and Ralph Benson – A.F.

Text copyright © 2001 by Anne Fine. Illustration copyright © 2001 by Ruth Brown
This paperback edition first published in 2003 by Andersen Press Ltd.
The rights of Anne Fine and Ruth Brown to be identified as the author and illustrator of this work
have been asserted by them in accordance with the Copyright, Designs and Patents Act, 1988.
First published in Great Britain in 2001 by Andersen Press Ltd. 20 Vauxhall Bridge Road, London SW1V 2SA.
Published in Australia by Random House Australia Pty., 20 Alfred Street, Milsons Point, Sydney, NSW 2061.
All rights reserved. Colour separated in Switzerland by Photolitho AG, Zürich.
Printed and bound in Italy by Grafiche AZ, Verona.

10 9 8 7 6 5 4 3

British Library Cataloguing in Publication Data available.

ISBN 1 84270 212 2

This book has been printed on acid-free paper

RUGGLES

story by Anne Fine   pictures by Ruth Brown

Ⓐ

Andersen Press

London

The gardener left the rabbit hutch by the fence.
Sue left the papers beside it.
The painter left a bucket . . .

. . . and I left home.

The dog lady spotted me
halfway down Acacia.
"Hi, Ruggles," she said.
"Off on your travels again?"

We both looked round.
It certainly was the most
beautiful spring day.
The air was fresh,
the clouds were spinning,
and little green whatsits
were sprouting all over.
We both enjoyed it for
a little while.

Then:
"OK, Ruggles," the dog lady told me.
"It's a bust. Get in the van."

Sue wasn't pleased. She went round looking at the fence. And at the ground. And at the locks on the gates.

"I can't imagine how it happened this time. You'd think two walks a day would be enough for an old man like him."

"Wouldn't you just?" said the dog lady. She winked at me. "Well, see you, Ruggles," she said cheerfully.

And I expect she will.

In summer it's easy, because
the only sensible paper boy goes off
to spend the holidays with his dad,
and the others don't bother to latch the gate
properly after them.

I bumped into Mr Tanner on my way to the river.
"Hi, Ruggles," he said. "Off fishing?"
I knew he'd just go home and snitch. So I went
round the other way, to the park.

It was a good choice.
Everyone was there.
The Fowler twins.
Marina Potts, with her sweet bag.

Mrs Dimaggio and Hugo Mackay.
Half the staff from the post office depot.
(They all know me.) And Hughie Venables.
The only boy on the planet who knows how
to scratch *exactly*, and just *there*.

Things buzzed and hummed around me.
The sun beat down. The flowers were lush,
and the trees in their splendour.
It was the perfect summer's day.
   Sometimes I sat and watched.
Sometimes I joined in and played.
Sometimes I sat again.
   Then I got hungry and went home for tea.

Whoops. Put my four great fat feet in it again.
I've made her wait for me. She makes me wait
for supper.

Come autumn, it's a doddle. You dig a really deep hole in the exact right place,

wait for a stiff gust of wind,
and, hey presto, guess what happens?
Down blows the Hendersons' lattice fence.

I went straight along to the shops.
I used to go to Harry's Meat Market,
but now I don't. I go next door
to the bakery. I find bread softer on the teeth.

Sue spotted me halfway up Linden Avenue.
I made a hasty left.
And then a right.
Then had a quick cower behind the Bensons'
dustbins. That shook her off.

I go back home in my own time . . .

. . . and she's not very pleased.
In fact she's furious.
She bawls me out,
sends me to my corner,
and won't even discuss
going out for my *real* walk.

I try not to worry. After all, you can't please everyone.
We all know that.

Winter's a breeze.
I reckon I could get out every day.
Shopping. Deliveries. Huge great umbrellas.
People in for drinks.

But damp gets in the old bones.
The pavements are wet. The trees are dripping,
and their trunks look dismal and slimy
even before I go past and make them
look worse.

Mind you,
it's impressive from *inside*.
Watch those leaves spin.

As for snow . . . well, that's so beautiful
it makes your heart sing. No point in being
a dog at all if you don't roll in fresh snow.
    And I defy anyone on earth to shovel their
path without leaving the gate open for
at least a few minutes.

But you can have too much adventuring. The trees are beckoning. The moon is scudding. And there's that strange silvery half-light over everything.

But it's so cosy here.
I will go back on my travels. It's in the blood.
But not right now. Not tonight.
Maybe next spring . . .